MY NAME IS KOFI

▼▼▼▼▼▼▼▼▼▼▼▼▼▼▼▼▼▼▼▼▼▼▼▼▼▼▼▼▼▼▼▼▼▼▼▼▼

Coming to America from Nigeria—1976

M. J. Cosson

SIPPS

SET 2

Perfection Learning®

Illustration: Jason Roe
Design: Tobi Cunningham

Acknowledgments

Many thanks to Yazomam Ugochukwu for your thoughtful review of this story.

For information, contact
Perfection Learning® Corporation
1000 North Second Avenue, P.O. Box 500
Logan, Iowa 51546-0500.
Phone: 1-800-831-4190 • Fax: 1-800-543-2745
perfectionlearning.com

PB ISBN-13: 978-0-7891-5519-1   ISBN-10: 0-7891-5519-2
RLB ISBN-13: 978-0-7569-0858-4   ISBN-10: 0-7569-0858-2
3 4 5 6 7 8 PP 16 15 14 13 12 11
PPI / 9 / 11

Table *of* Contents

Introduction

▼▼▼▼▼

Nigeria in 1976

In olden days, different peoples ruled the various parts of Nigeria. The **Yoruba** people lived in the rain forests of the southwest. They built cities, such as Ife and Benin.

The **Ibo** people farmed **yams** in the forests east of the Niger Delta. They lived in villages governed by a council of elders.

The **Fulani** people were wanderers. They lived in northern Nigeria. They expanded their empire through conquest.

In the west, the **Hausa** people built seven city-states. They traded with the Arabs. In time, many Hausa people began to practice the Arabs' Islam religion.

By the 1400s, Europeans were coming to Africa. They traded metal tools, cooking utensils, cloth, and glass for the gold, ivory, and spices of Africa.

By 1480, European colonies in North and South America needed workers for sugar, tobacco, rice, **indigo**, and cotton **plantations**. The slave trade began. Over the centuries, 20 to 30 million African people were taken as slaves.

By the early 19th century, the British had made it illegal to sell slaves to the United States. Britain had lost the North American colonies. So they began to colonize Africa.

At the beginning of the 20th century, Nigeria was under British rule. By the 1920s, many Yoruba, Ibo, and Hausa peoples thought of themselves as Nigerians.

Two parties were formed to free
Nigeria from British rule. One was
the Nigerian National Democratic
Party (NNDP). The followers of
Nnamdi Azikiwe, known as Zik of
Africa, made up the other group.

The NNDP pushed for free
education and more voice in the
government. Zik's followers called
for **boycotts** and **strikes**. Riots
and looting broke out.

Finally in 1960, Britain gave up
rule. Nigeria declared itself
independent on October 1, 1960.

Nigeria became a republic in
1963. However, independence did
not solve all the problems. The
Hausa, Ibo, and Yoruba people
fought over who should control the
country.

In 1966, the military took over.
Matters did not improve. Ten
thousand Ibo people were killed.

This caused many Ibos to **migrate** back to their native eastern region.

In 1967, the Ibo people broke away from Nigeria. They formed a new nation called the Republic of **Biafra**. The civil war lasted for two and a half years. Over two million Nigerians died. Many of the people in Biafra starved to death. When Biafra **surrendered**, Nigeria again became one nation.

Nigeria has many languages. These include Fulani, Ibo, Yoruba, and Hausa. But the official language of Nigeria is English.

In 1976, Nigeria still had a military government. The nation's oil wealth helped them rebuild. But many problems remained. Nigerians still hoped for democracy.

United States in 1976

The year 1976 was a turning point for African Americans in the United States. It was also the United States' bicentennial. The U.S. had been a democratic nation for 200 years.

A few years earlier, Congress had passed the Civil Rights Act. It promised equality for people of all races. Other legislation followed that further defined civil rights.

A presidential election took place in November of 1976. A record number of African Americans voted in that election. They helped elect Jimmy Carter as president.

At the Democratic National Convention earlier that year, Shirley Chisholm had been a candidate. Ms. Chisholm was a congresswoman from New York. She was the first African American woman to seek the presidential nomination from a major political party.

Representative Barbara Jordan of Texas was another African American woman. She was a **keynote speaker** at the Democratic National Convention. Here is part of what she said.

> There is something different and special about this opening night. I am a keynote speaker.
>
> In the interesting years since 1832, it would have been most unusual for any national political party to have asked a Barbara Jordan to make a keynote address—most unusual.

The past notwithstanding,
a Barbara Jordan is before
you tonight. This is one
additional bit of evidence
that the American dream
need not forever be
deferred. . . .

One of President John F.
Kennedy's contributions to society
was the Peace Corps. The Peace
Corps is an organization that sends
volunteers from the United States to
other countries. The volunteers have
special training in fields such as
engineering, teaching, or medicine.
These volunteers teach and help
people in the other countries.

Congress passed the Peace Corps
Act on September 22, 1961. By
December of 1974, the Peace Corps
was serving in 69 countries. At the
close of the seventies, more than
6,000 Peace Corps volunteers were

at work in the field.

President Jimmy Carter was another great **advocate** of the Peace Corps. His mother, Ms. Lillian Carter, had been a Peace Corps volunteer. She had served as a nurse in India during the late 1960s.

Coming *to* America
from Nigeria
1976

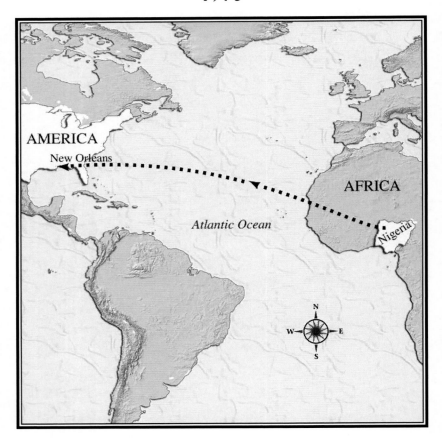

1

The Agreement

"Why must I go?" Kofi asked. Tears sparkled in his gray eyes.

"Because of the agreement," his mother said. "You know that. It's not what I want for myself. It is what I want for you. Your father and I both want it for you."

Kofi's mother hugged him tightly. Then she turned him around. She shoved him gently through the doorway.

"Go!" she said. "I love you!" she yelled as Kofi walked down the hallway.

Kofi boarded the airplane. He found his seat near the back.

He sat down and peered out the window. Waves of heat made the runway look like water. In a few minutes, the plane would rise into the air.

Kofi had never been on a plane before. Now he was going far away.

Kofi tried to find his mother in the airport windows. It was dark inside the airport. All he could see was the reflection of his plane. He waved anyway.

"Is your seat belt on?" the flight attendant asked.

Kofi shook his head. He reached down and found his seat belt. He pushed one piece into the other until it clicked.

The lady nodded. "Please keep that on. I'll let you know when you can take it off."

Kofi wondered why he needed the seat belt. He was going up in the air, not forward. In a car, you wore a seat belt to keep yourself from flying around in a crash. But if the airplane crashed, he didn't think the seat belt would be much help.

Why must I go to America? Kofi thought. He had known about the agreement for a long time. He had worried about it. But he never believed it would happen. He thought his mother loved him more than that.

Kofi remembered when his mother had first told him about the agreement.

"You know your father lives in the United States," she had said.

Kofi had nodded. He received letters and gifts from his father. His father sent pictures too. But Kofi didn't remember him. Kofi's father had gone back to the U.S. when Kofi was a baby.

"I get you for the first 11 years of your life," his mother had said. "Your father gets you for the next ten years. When you are 21, you will be an adult. Then you can choose. You can come back to Nigeria. Or you can stay in the United States."

They should have just sliced me in half, Kofi thought. Half here, half there. Instead, they sliced my life in half.

Now Kofi was flying to the United States. He would spend the next ten years with a father he didn't know—a white father.

2

▼▼▼▼▼

Kofi's Father

Jim Nelson was Kofi's father. In 1963, he had finished college with a degree in English. He had wanted to do some good in the world. So he joined the Peace Corps. In 1964, he was sent to Nigeria to teach English.

Jim taught at the Calabar Secondary School. A young woman taught other classes. Her name was Emotan.

Jim had other jobs besides teaching the students. He helped other teachers learn to teach better. He gave Emotan new ideas about teaching. They spent time after school talking about teaching.

Jim and Emotan had shared many interests. They both felt that education was the answer to Nigeria's problems.

They enjoyed the rain forest—but not during the monsoons or big dust storms.

They mostly enjoyed talking over a meal. Yams, mangoes, and papayas were their favorite foods. Jim and Emotan became friends. Their friendship grew. Soon, they had fallen in love.

Jim and Emotan were married in Calabar. In 1965, Emotan had a baby boy. They named him Kofi Nelson.

When Jim's **tour** was up, he stayed in Nigeria with his family. He had planned to sign up for another two-year tour with the Peace Corps. But Jim came down with malaria. He was too sick to support his wife and child.

Then the civil war began. Danger was everywhere. Jim had begged Emotan to come to the United States with him.

Emotan would not leave her family and her country. She said good-bye to Jim Nelson. But she would not let him take her baby.

"Kofi will be safe with me," she said. This made Jim very angry. But he could do nothing.

Jim and Emotan were divorced. Then Jim returned to the United States alone.

Before Jim left, he and Emotan had made the agreement. Jim would go back to the United States. He would get well and find a job. He would send money to help support Kofi. Then when Kofi turned 11, Emotan would send the boy to the United States.

So Jim had returned to the United States. He began teaching English at a high school. He went back to college. He became an English professor at Tulane University in New Orleans, Louisiana.

Jim married again. His new wife, Ann, was a professor at Tulane too. She taught African Studies. Jim and Ann had two children.

Over the years, Jim sent presents to Kofi. He sent pictures of his family. But he didn't visit. Kofi knew he had a sister named Kate who was five. He also had a sister named

Sara. She was three.

Kofi would now live with Jim, Ann, Kate, and Sara. He would live in a house with four white people he did not know.

Kofi knew that long ago people from his country had gone to the United States. They had been slaves. Slave traders bought or captured them. The traders put the slaves on ships that sailed to North and South America.

Once there, the slaves were sold to plantation owners. The slaves worked in the cotton or sugarcane fields.

I'm just another slave, Kofi thought. Jim Nelson has captured me. My mother sold me to him. He doesn't love me like I thought my mother did. He doesn't even know me. Why would he want me? I'll be his slave.

The plane took off. Kofi felt it lift up, up into the air. He looked out the window. He saw the buildings of his town grow smaller and smaller. Quickly, they disappeared.

Next Kofi saw a white haze out the window. Soon he could see nothing. His town was gone. His country was gone. Kofi was in the clouds.

Kofi had been afraid to fly. But now he began to relax. It didn't seem much different than riding in a car. He took off his seat belt.

BUMP! The plane hit a pocket of **turbulence**. It took a big dip. Kofi's head hit the ceiling. He had never felt such pain. Then everything went dark.

3
▼▼▼▼▼

The Dark

Kofi lay in the blackness. He tried to see, but it was dark. Moving was impossible.

People were close to him on both sides. He could feel their skin next to his. Something was holding his feet down. He tried to lift his feet. He felt heavy weights around his ankles.

"Where am I?" Kofi cried.

"Hush, child," the voice on his left said.

Kofi tried to stand up. He couldn't. A hand tapped his leg.

"Be still," the voice on his right said. "You know what happens if you make trouble."

"What happens?" Kofi asked.

"They take you away. Be still. Soon there will be food."

Kofi lay still. His mind raced. This wasn't the airplane. Had it crashed? Where were his clothes? Why did he feel a rocking movement?

"Where are we?" he asked. No one answered.

"Where are we?" he asked again.

"You know as well as I do," the voice on his left whispered. "Don't you remember? They tricked us. They chased us into the water. All we could do was walk onto this ship. Are you sick, boy?"

"Yes," Kofi said. "My head hurts."

"Lie still. If they know you're sick, they'll get rid of you."

Kofi lay as still as he could. He slept for a while. When he awoke, a bright square of light was shining down on him. A door shut. The light was gone.

"Where are we going?" Kofi asked.

"I don't know," the voice on his right said.

"I heard one of the men say to America," the voice on his left said.

"Oh, yes," Kofi said. "I know. Now I remember."

4
▼▼▼▼▼

The Pen

All Kofi could do was sleep. Each
time he woke up, he thought he'd be
on the plane again. But each time, Kofi
was still in the dark.

Every so often, the people were allowed to get up. They'd have a few minutes to stretch.

For meals, they were given clamshells filled with **gruel**. The clamshells were dished up and passed down the line. After they ate the gruel, they were given water.

This food tastes real, Kofi thought. This is a long dream. But soon I will wake up.

Every day, the door opened. And many days, someone was taken out. Kofi would see the people against the square of light. Two white men and a black person. Sometimes the men carried the black person. Sometimes the black person was fighting to get free.

"They'll dump him in the ocean," the voice next to him said. "If he's not dead yet, he soon will be."

One day, the rocking motion was different. It felt as if the ship had stopped moving forward. The bright square of light shone down. A man stood in the doorway yelling to the people below. Kofi did not understand his words. The people began to stand.

Kofi watched the lines of chained people move out the door. Soon his line was allowed to follow. They walked slowly toward the door. The bright light made his eyes ache. It seemed like many weeks since he had seen daylight.

Kofi was led off the ship. He was **shackled** to the person in front of him and behind him. For the first time, Kofi could see the people near him. He did not know them. They also did not seem to know him.

The sun shone down on the people as they were led off the ship.

It felt good to Kofi to be in the sun again.

What a dream! I'm a slave, Kofi thought. I was telling myself I would be a slave. And now I am one!

Kofi looked around. He saw buildings made of wood or stone. In the distance, an open-air marketplace was swarming with people. Horses pranced down the street pulling buggies. Well-dressed white people rode in the buggies.

The slaves were herded into pens. There they waited, not knowing what the future held. Because they were still shackled together, Kofi could only go where everyone else went. At least there was room in the pens for them to sit down.

People walked by the pens. They looked at the slaves. Some pointed and laughed.

I'm like an animal in a zoo, Kofi thought.

Before night fell, the slaves were given some food. They received bread, water, and scraps of fat meat.

"Eat up," the man who fed them said. "We want you to look healthy and well-fed for the auction tomorrow."

5

▼▼▼▼

The Auction

The white men took a few slaves at a
time out of the pen. Those who left the
pen never returned. By mid-morning, it
was Kofi's turn to go.

Kofi watched the sale of the woman in front of him. She stood naked on the auction block. He could see her shiver. Was she cold, afraid, or ashamed?

Probably all three, Kofi thought.

"Fellow citizens, here is a fine black girl. She will be a strong worker. And she will bear many children. What am I offered for her?"

"Two hundred," someone yelled.

"Two fifty!"

"Three hundred!"

The bidding went on until the final price of $800 was reached.

"Sold!" the auctioneer yelled.

The woman was taken from the auction block. Kofi was led onto it.

"This young black buck is thin now. But he will grow into a fine field hand. Give him a couple of years to fill out. I wager he'll be your best worker. What's the bid?"

"Fifty dollars," someone said.

"Seventy-five. It'll cost me money to fatten him up."

"One hundred."

"This boy is worth more than that!" the auctioneer said. "In no time, you'll have yourself a fine strong man. Offer me what he's worth."

"Right now he's worth no more than two hundred," a big man in a black hat said. "I'm not buying him in the future. I'm buying him right now."

"Sold!" the auctioneer said.

Kofi was hauled off the auction block. He was turned over to the man in the black hat.

The man pointed to Kofi. "You Robert. Say 'me Robert.' "

Kofi just stared at the man.

"Say it!" the man demanded. He took out his buggy whip. He held it over Kofi.

"Me Robert," Kofi said.

"You aren't so dumb. You're just stubborn." The man whipped Kofi's back lightly with the whip. It stung.

"You remember that," the man said. "Now you belong to me. You remember who you are. And you remember who's the boss."

Someone had taken the chains off Kofi's feet. The man put a rope around Kofi's wrists and led him to a wagon. Four other slaves were tied to the wagon. The man went back to the auction.

"What's your name?" one of the other slaves asked.

"Kofi."

"Didn't he give you a new name?" the other slave asked.

"My name is Kofi."

"You need a new name. My name is Joe. This here is Andrew. She's Mary. And he's Frank." The man pointed to the others.

"My name is Kofi," Kofi said.
Nobody was going to change his name,
even if it was only a dream.

6
▼▼▼▼

The Plantation

By dusk, Kofi and the others were on the plantation. They had walked the eight miles from New Orleans. The master had driven the wagon with all the slaves tied to the back.

At least he drove it slow, Kofi thought. His bare feet were bleeding. He was not used to walking so far. He noticed that the other slaves' feet were not bleeding.

I wonder why their feet are so tough, Kofi thought.

Kofi sat down on the ground. He looked at his sore feet. He could feel the cuts as if they were real.

"Stand up!" the master said. Kofi stood.

"Mind you do what I say, boy. Or you'll be whipped." The master pointed his buggy whip at Kofi.

Kofi nodded. But that is not what he wanted to say. He wanted to say, "Why can you tell me what to do?" He didn't need to ask the question though. He already knew the answer.

Small shacks lined the plantation road. People stood outside the shacks. They stared at the new arrivals.

"This is Mack Smith, your **overseer**," the master said. He untied the slaves from the wagon. "Mind him or you'll answer to us both."

The master climbed back into his wagon. He rode off toward the big house.

Mack Smith spoke. "You are the property of Mr. William Harmon. He is your master. You will always do what he or I tell you to do. If you don't, you will get a beating. Sometimes I will give it to you. Sometimes he will. It will be worse if the master gives you a beating. He only beats his slaves when he is mad. I've seen him beat a man to death."

Mack pulled one of the men from in front of a cabin. He pulled up the man's **homespun** shirt. His back was crossed with scars.

"This doesn't look as bad as it feels, does it, Luke?"

The slave shook his head. "No, sir," he said.

"If you try to run away, the **patrollers** will catch you. They'll bring you back. The master will beat you. Believe me, you don't want to make the master mad."

Mack walked from slave to slave. He looked each new slave in the eye. Then he nodded. "This isn't a bad place if you do your work and mind your master."

The people in front of the log cabins seemed to be families. Mack divided the new slaves into families. He put Kofi into a cabin with Andrew and Mary. Andrew was tall and thin. Mary was short and heavy.

What an odd family I have, Kofi thought.

Their small cabin had a fireplace for cooking. It was made of mud and sticks. It looked like it would catch fire and burn easily.

Kofi slept on a pallet on the floor. He hadn't slept much since he came off the boat. His sleep that night was deep.

7

The Cotton Fields

A wonderful surprise awaited Kofi the next morning. Breakfast! Kofi followed Mary and Andrew to the cookhouse.

Hot fresh bread with molasses made Kofi's mouth water. He gobbled it up. He had fried potatoes and fried salt meat dipped in cornmeal. It seemed ages since Kofi had eaten so well. It made him dizzy to think about it.

When the field hands were full, they were led to the cotton fields. Some fields grew cotton already. Kofi helped clear land to plant more cotton. He spent the morning digging, pulling, hauling, and making piles to burn. By noon, Kofi was tired and hungry.

Lunch was good too. Women brought the food to the fields. Kofi ate two baked potatoes. He had hot **corn pone**, boiled pork, and a baked onion. He drank water to wash down his meal.

All afternoon and evening, Kofi worked in the fields. He had never worked so hard in his life. By nightfall, he was almost too tired to eat. That night he had fried fish, **collard greens**, and **hoecakes**.

Kofi fell asleep right after supper. He was sore all over. His cut feet still hurt. But his aching muscles made him forget his sore feet. Kofi didn't wake up until Andrew pulled him out of bed the next morning.

The days became routine. The food was rarely as good as it had been the first day. Many days the slaves shared big bowls of bread, milk, and mush. But Kofi always had enough to eat.

8
▼▼▼▼▼

My Name Is Kofi

One hot afternoon, the master came
out to the fields. He wanted to see how
the clearing of the new fields was
going. He rode a fine-looking horse.

Kofi was digging out a tree stump. The land was swampy. Kofi's bare feet sank into the mud.

In the time he had been there, Kofi had developed tough soles on his feet. The cuts had long since healed. Kofi had also developed muscles. The auctioneer had been right. Kofi was a good worker.

The master rode his horse near Kofi.

"You're getting strong, Robert," the master said. He smiled as he thought of his good purchase. This boy would make a fine slave.

Kofi did not look up. He kept on working.

"I spoke to you, Robert," the master said.

Kofi did not mean to be rude. He had forgotten that the master had named him Robert. He had told all the slaves that his name was Kofi. That's what they had been calling him.

The master climbed off his horse. He took his whip from the saddle and walked close to Kofi.

"I spoke to you, Robert," the master said again.

This time, Kofi looked up. He looked the master in the eye. He saw the anger there. He remembered that the master had given him a new name. But he could not make himself answer to the name Robert.

"My name is Kofi."

The master's face turned red. His eyes bulged. The veins in his neck stood out. He spit as he yelled, "Your name is Robert. Say it!"

Kofi would do this man's work. But he would not let this man name him.

"My name is Kofi."

The master drew back on the whip. He brought it down on Kofi's back. It stung like a hundred wasp stings.

Kofi did not cry out.

The master drew back on the whip again. And again. And again. And again.

Kofi's homespun shirt was ripped to shreds. Blood oozed down his back. Yet he did not cry out.

Kofi, he said to himself. My name is Kofi.

Kofi fell to the ground. He no longer felt the sting of the whip. He no longer felt anything. He had passed out from the pain.

9
▼▼▼▼▼

The Right Answer

Kofi opened his eyes. His back did not hurt now. But his head ached very badly. A white woman was leaning over him.

"How do you feel?" she asked.

"Are you the lady of the plantation?" Kofi asked. He hoped the master's wife was kinder than the master.

"No, I'm the flight attendant," she said. "You had a bad bump on your head. Do you remember when I told you that you should not unfasten your seat belt until I said so? The plane hit an air pocket. You had unfastened your seat belt. You flew up and bumped your head on the ceiling. You've been out for some time. We were worried. I'm so glad you're awake now.

"Once we get to New Orleans, you'll need to see a doctor. An ambulance will be waiting to take you to the hospital."

Kofi closed his eyes. It was a dream, he thought. How real it seemed.

"Can you stay awake until we get there?" the flight attendant asked. "Let me get you something to drink. You must be thirsty."

"I am. Thank you," Kofi said. He was very thirsty. And he was hungry. He was hot. His head ached. All of his muscles ached too.

I feel like I've been working in the hot sun, Kofi thought. I feel like I've been clearing fields for cotton crops.

The flight attendant brought a glass of ginger ale.

"Sip slowly through the straw," she said. "You'd better not eat until you've seen a doctor."

As soon as the plane landed, a man in a white jacket boarded. He rushed back to Kofi. He ran his fingers over Kofi's head and neck. He looked in Kofi's eyes. "Can you tell me your name?" he asked.

What's the right answer? Kofi

thought for a moment.

"My name is Kofi," he said. "Kofi Nelson."

10

▼▼▼▼▼

Getting Checked Out

Kofi was taken off the plane in a
wheelchair. When he reached the
terminal, he saw four familiar faces—
faces he'd only seen in pictures.

Jim Nelson rushed up to his son. Tears streamed down his cheeks. He reached out to hug and touch Kofi. His wife and children were right behind him.

"Better save that for later," the man in the white jacket said. "There will be plenty of time for hugs after we've examined him."

"I'm coming with you in the ambulance," Jim said. He turned to his wife. "The flight attendant will help you get Kofi's bags. Take the girls home. I'll call you from the hospital," he said.

The man quickly wheeled Kofi through the airport. Jim walked alongside. The ambulance was waiting outside a door. The man in the white jacket put Kofi into the ambulance.

"You'll have to ride up front," he told Jim. Then the attendant climbed in back with Kofi.

On the way to the hospital, the man checked Kofi's vital signs. At the hospital, a doctor examined Kofi.

Kofi was placed into a big machine. The machine took pictures of his brain.

"This is very strange," the doctor said. "It appears that nothing is wrong. I can't find any evidence of even a bump on the head. How does your head feel?"

"It feels fine now," Kofi said. "My ears feel funny though."

"That's normal," the doctor said. "That's from flying. You need to swallow a lot when you go up or come down in a plane. It helps clear your ears."

The doctor shook his head. "I don't understand why you were out for so long," he said.

I was being a slave, Kofi thought.

"Can he go home now?" Jim asked the doctor.

"I don't see why not," the doctor said. He told Jim to keep Kofi quiet and call if there was any change.

11
▼▼▼▼▼

The Ride Home

Jim finally could give Kofi a hug.
"Do you have any idea how much I've
longed for this minute?" Jim asked.

Kofi backed away and looked at his dad. He looked into gray eyes that matched his own. His father's eyes said more than words could say. Kofi could tell that his idea of being a slave was just a dream.

Jim led Kofi to the main entrance. He signaled a waiting cab. The two climbed into the backseat.

They drove from the hospital through New Orleans.

"We live in a newer section of town," Jim said. "Your sisters and Ann are anxious for me to bring you home."

They passed Tulane University where Kofi's father worked. Jim pointed to some of the big old houses near the university.

"Some of these houses are very old," he said. "There are old plantations nearby too. One day, I'll take you to visit some. We'll also go to the French Quarter. That's old New Orleans."

"Is there a market there?" Kofi asked.

"Yes, there are many shops, and there's an open-air market too. It's been there for a long, long time," his dad said.

Kofi looked at his dad. "Did they sell slaves there?"

Jim looked at Kofi out of the corner of his eye. "Yes, they did. I can show you where they sold slaves, if you're interested."

Kofi nodded. He settled back in the seat.

Jim reached over. He put his hand on Kofi's shoulder.

"I'm sorry I haven't come to Nigeria to see you," he said. "I wanted to. At first, I didn't have the money. Also your mom and I were not on very good terms. I was very angry at her for not agreeing to come with me. It took me years to get over it."

Jim paused. "This is pretty grown-up stuff, I know. But I feel like I need to tell you why I haven't seen you. Your mother would not allow you to come here until now. I think she was afraid you wouldn't come home.

"I'm sure your mom is still hoping that you will insist on going back to Nigeria soon. Please give it a chance here. I want you to stay. You are my only son. I have so much to teach you."

Kofi looked at his dad. Were those tears in his eyes again? Or was the wind making his eyes water?

Kofi looked at New Orleans. The last time I was here—when I was a slave—it was much smaller, he thought.

12
▼▼▼▼▼

Welcome Home

The cab pulled into the driveway of a two-story brick house. A banner was draped across the front of the house. It said "Welcome Home, Kofi."

In the driveway sat an old red Ford Mustang. Kofi's dad had sent him pictures of it. Jim had also sent Kofi some picture books about cars. Kofi knew a lot about American cars. He loved cars, just as his dad did.

The front door opened. Ann, Kate, and Sara came out. They held hands as they walked toward the cab.

When Kofi climbed out, Ann let go of the girls' hands. She stepped forward and gave Kofi a big hug.

"I'm so glad to finally meet you," Ann said. "Your father and I have been planning this moment for years now."

That's what he said too, Kofi thought. It must be true.

"Hi, Kofi," Kate said. She gave Kofi a polite hug.

"Hi, Kofi," Sara said. She also gave Kofi a hug.

"Where have you been?" Sara asked.

"In Nigeria," Kofi said.

"Did you fly here from there? Or did you stop someplace on the way?" Sara asked.

"I flew here from there," Kofi said. He didn't remember stopping anywhere but New Orleans. He didn't tell Sara that his first stop was at least 150 years earlier.

"Did you know you're our brother?" Sara asked.

"You don't have to answer all Sara's questions," Kate said. "It will only make her ask more. Just ignore her."

Kofi looked at Sara and Kate. "I don't mind answering questions," he said. "It's fun."

Sara smiled. She took Kofi's hand and led him into the house. It smelled wonderful inside. Kofi's stomach growled.

"This is the living room," Sara said. The whole family walked Kofi around the downstairs. The dining room table was set. When they went into the kitchen, bowls and pans of food were everywhere.

"We've made a nice dinner," Jim said. "We'll eat when you're ready."

"I'm starving," Kofi said. When had he last eaten? Was it lunch on the plantation?

It was a long time ago! Kofi thought.

"Let me just finish a couple of things. Then we'll eat," Ann said. "Jim will you help me?"

The girls took Kofi upstairs. They showed him their rooms. They showed him their parents' room.

"And this room is yours," Kate said. She opened a door. Kofi walked in. Two big windows looked down on the street. The room was painted blue. There was a bed, a desk, a dresser, and a chair. Pictures of old cars hung on the walls. On the dresser was a framed picture of Kofi's mother and father when they were much younger. They were holding a baby boy.

That's me, Kofi thought.

"Do you like the room?" Sara asked.

Kofi nodded. His bags sat beside the closet.

"You can unpack later. Let's go eat," Kate said. "We're having turkey, like at Thanksgiving. And Mom made an apple pie for dessert. We can put ice cream on top."

Sara, Kate, and Kofi ran downstairs.

"After dinner, we'll call your mom. I know she's anxious to know you arrived here all right," Ann said.

"Boy," Jim sighed. "It sure feels good to have you with us." He looked at Kofi. "I thought this day would never get here."

Kofi thought about his mother. He missed her very much. But he knew now that she wanted what was best for him.

Kofi remembered the master, Mr. Harmon. He had been a mean man.

Had he really lived? Kofi wondered.

Or had he only lived in my mind?

Kofi looked around the table. Already he loved his sisters. Ann was very nice. Kofi felt her love.

Kofi put his arm on the table, next to Jim's. Their hands were the same shape.

There's a lot of my dad in me, Kofi thought. I want to get to know him better. I know how I am like my mom. Now I want to know how I am like my dad.

Kofi looked at his skin color next to his father's. He looked across the table at Ann. Her skin was darker than Jim's. Was she African American too? Kofi couldn't tell.

Sara was looking at her father's arm next to Kofi's. "Your arm is like the dark meat in the turkey," she said to Kofi, holding up her drumstick. "And Dad's skin is like the white meat."

Everyone laughed.

"Welcome to your other home, son," Jim said. "You may get homesick, but there will always be something to laugh about."

Kofi smiled. It won't be so bad here, now that it's 1976, he thought. In fact, I think I'll like it.

Glossary

advocate person who supports a cause

Biafra bee-AF-rah

boycott act of refusing to do business with or to associate with a person or organization

collard green smooth-leaved plant related to cabbage

corn pone baked or fried corn bread made without milk or eggs

defer   put off;
                   postpone

Fulani   foo-LAHN-ee

gruel   a thin cooked
                   cereal

Hausa   HOW-sa

hoecake   small cake
                   made from
                   cornmeal

homespun   simple; made by
                   hand

Ibo   EE-boh

indigo   plant used for
                   its deep reddish
                   blue color

keynote speaker	person who presents the primary issues to an assembly. This person usually brings unity and enthusiasm to the group.
migrate	to move from one place to another
overseer	manager; supervisor
patroller	person who is sent out to capture escaped slaves

plantation

large farm owned by one family but worked by others who live there

shackle

to chain together

strike

work stoppage

surrender

to give up to another, such as to end a war

tour

time period in which one performs a specific duty

turbulence	air that is gusty and unstable, causing planes to rise or drop without warning
yam	orange root vegetable similar to a sweet potato
Yoruba	YAW-ruh-buh